JOURNEY

Based on the True Story of OR7

THE MOST FAMOUS WOLF
IN THE WEST

Emma Bland Smith   *Illustrated by* **Robin James**

little bigfoot

an imprint of sasquatch books
seattle, wa

The wolf took one last look at his mother and his father. This
sweet-smelling forest of pines and firs had always been home. But
he was grown now. Most of his brothers and sisters had already
left to start their own families. It was time for him to do the same.

He began to walk slowly away. If he stayed close to home in these
woods that he knew so well, life would be easier.

But as he peered into the distance, he felt an unexpected thrill.
What was out there? What lay past the mountains?

He walked faster into the unknown.

The Daily News

California Bound?

First wolf in Western Oregon since 1945!

Abby pulled herself onto a stool at the diner.

Some ranchers at the next table were talking. "Did you see this? There's a wolf headed our way!"

Abby and her dad read the article the ranchers were talking about. They learned that a long time ago there had been wolves all over the country.

"Were there really wolves here before?" Abby asked her dad.

"Yes," he said. "There were thousands of wolves here in Northern California."

They continued to read the article and learned that biologists were trying to reintroduce these magnificent animals to areas where there are vast stretches of wilderness, not too many roads, and not too many farms—just right for wolves.

Then, about a year ago, something happened: a wolf in Northern Oregon—OR7—left his pack, crossed a mountain range, and was now traveling steadily southward.

"Oh, I hope he'll come to California," said Abby. But she guessed that was unlikely.

The wolf stepped over some fallen trees. His sharp ears heard a low click, and he turned his head toward the noise.

His powerful nose caught a lingering scent of humans. His tail dropped down and he froze. The humans weren't here now—his senses told him that. But they had been, not too long ago.

He veered away sharply and headed into the dense woods.

Abby froze with her spoonful of cereal halfway to her mouth. The wolf stared out at her from the television screen—the first photo of him ever.

"So that's what he looks like!" Abby thought.

The photo had been snapped by a hunter's hidden motion-sensor camera near Butte Falls, in Southern Oregon, just thirty-eight miles from the California border.

"Dad, look!" Abby said happily. She turned and grinned at her dad, but he wasn't grinning back.

"That poor fella better be careful," Dad said quietly.

Abby's smile disappeared as her dad explained that while most people were excited to welcome back this shy visitor, others thought that the wolf would hunt their sheep or cows, and that it should be chased away—or worse.

Abby was so worried she could barely sleep that night.

MORNING NEWS...

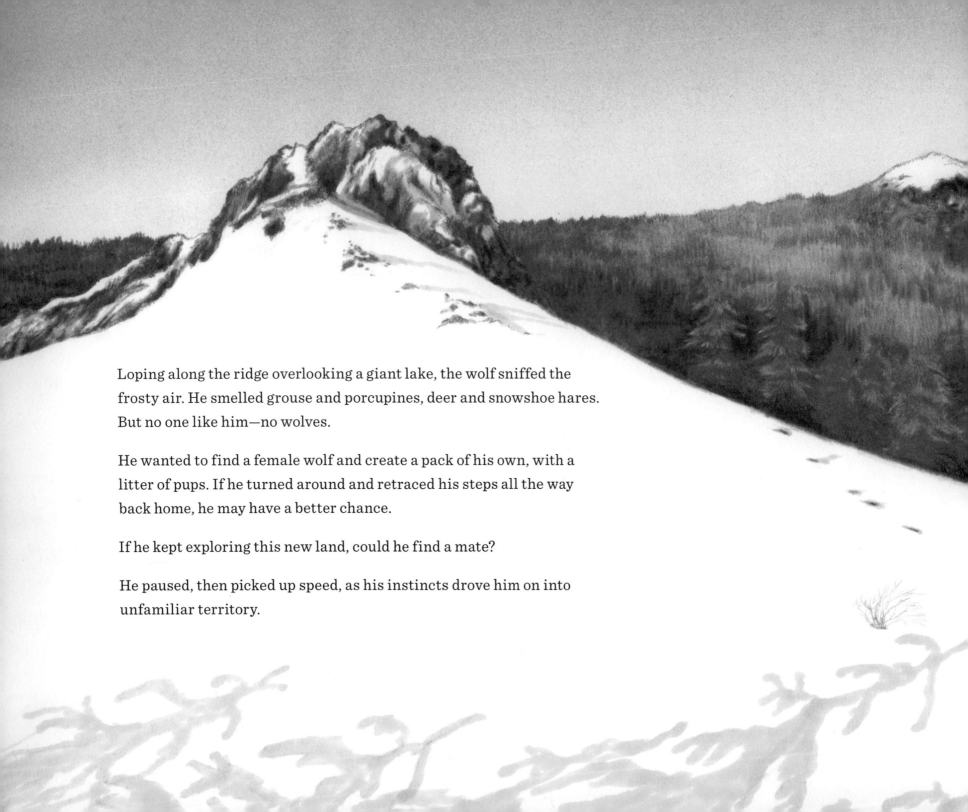

Loping along the ridge overlooking a giant lake, the wolf sniffed the
frosty air. He smelled grouse and porcupines, deer and snowshoe hares.
But no one like him—no wolves.

He wanted to find a female wolf and create a pack of his own, with a
litter of pups. If he turned around and retraced his steps all the way
back home, he may have a better chance.

If he kept exploring this new land, could he find a mate?

He paused, then picked up speed, as his instincts drove him on into
unfamiliar territory.

"He crossed the border!" Abby could hardly believe it.

For weeks now she had been following the wolf's route on the internet. The last update said he had been near Crater Lake in Oregon. Today she'd learned that he had finally made it into California, becoming the first wolf in the state in almost one hundred years!

Excitedly she stuck a new thumbtack into the map on her wall.

Going back to the computer, she scrolled down on the screen and read comments from other readers. Many people were happy about the wolf. But others were afraid, and that fear was turning to anger.

"That wolf better keep away from my farm, or else," one comment read.

Abby knew what that meant. The wolf was in danger.

Was there anything she could do to help?

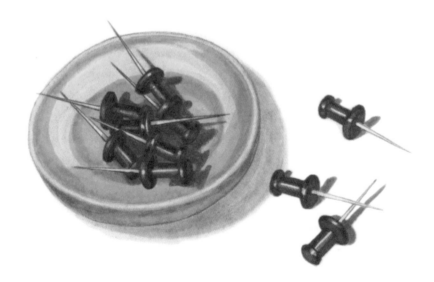

The wolf pushed on, weaving around boulders dotting the fields.

As he traveled, the sun rose over the enormous mountain, and meadows gave way to forests. Deer grazed, froze, then fled, and rabbits zigzagged wildly through the thickets.

This was good land. Wolf country. But where were the other wolves?

Wolves live better in packs, not alone. Hunting is more difficult alone. Sleeping is more dangerous alone. The wolf had to find a companion . . . and soon.

"A contest to name the wolf!" cried Abby, listening to a local radio broadcast. A conservation group was asking children to send in suggestions. This could be her chance to help him. She got out her notebook and pencil.

Brownie? No.

Cal, for California? No.

Spot? No.

Orrie, for Oregon? Maybe.

She thought for hours. And then it came to her.

One day, after he'd left the mountains for the flat, dry plains, the wolf spotted an animal in the distance, racing through the sagebrush. Two of them. Three. A whole pack. Not quite wolves, though—coyotes.

He quivered with excitement. Shyly, he introduced himself, and they ran together. Could he make a pack with these creatures?

"Abby," called Dad. "It's for you!"

"Hello?" Abby wasn't used to getting phone calls. Her confused look became a smile as she turned to her dad and said, "They chose Journey! They chose my name!"

After that the news spread like wildfire. Within days the whole world seemed to know about Journey the wolf.

That week Abby's teacher taught a lesson on gray wolves. Her cousins in New York called to say they'd read about Journey in the paper. Even her grandparents, far away in Mexico, heard the news.

Journey was famous—too famous to harm, just as the contest organizers had planned. Abby hoped he would be safe now.

Back in her room Abby studied her map. The trail of thumbtacks showed that Journey had turned around. He was still in California, but heading north. And that made Abby nervous. Would Journey stay here or head back? Now, all over the world, people were watching, listening, and hoping.

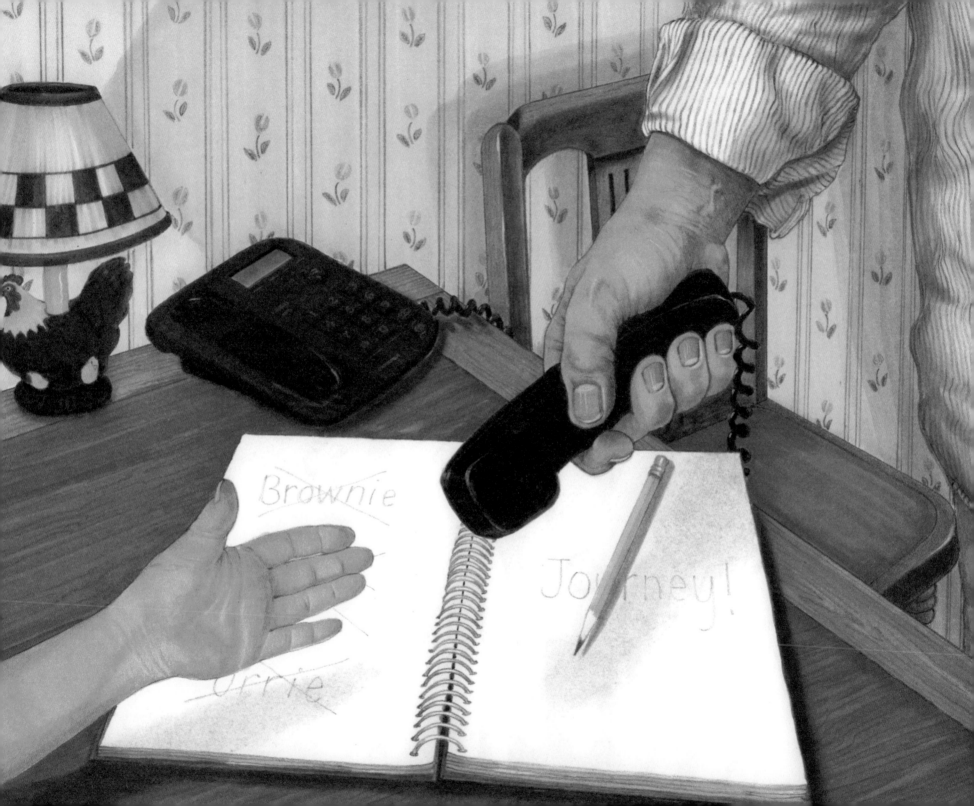

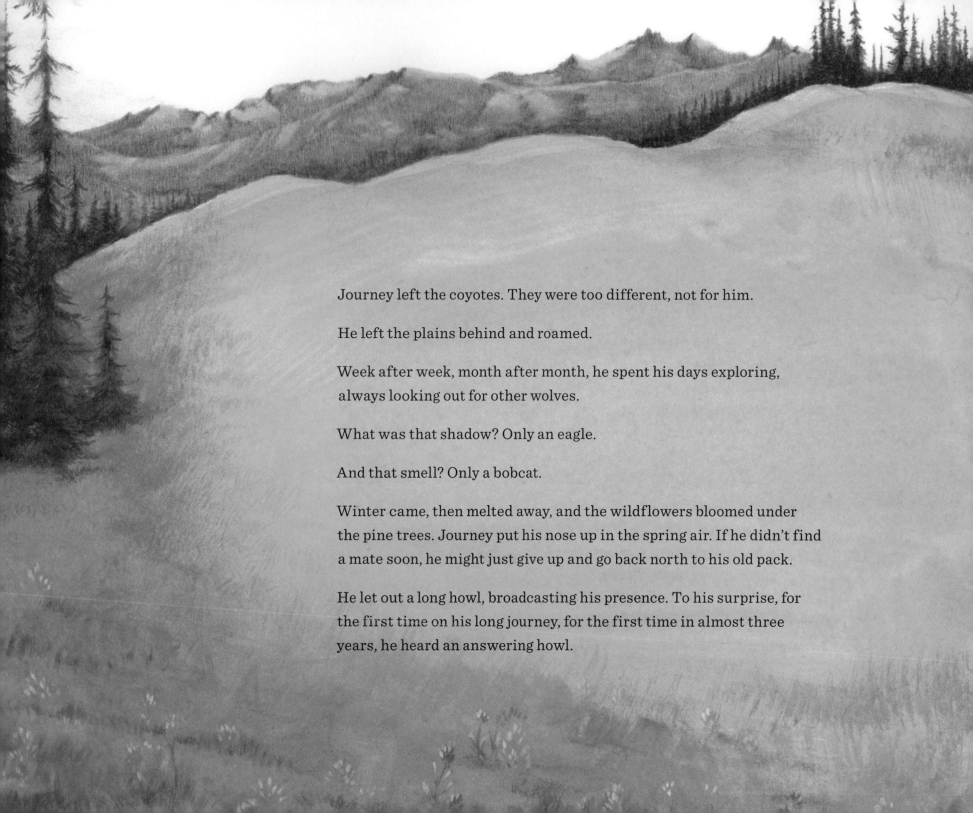

Journey left the coyotes. They were too different, not for him.

He left the plains behind and roamed.

Week after week, month after month, he spent his days exploring, always looking out for other wolves.

What was that shadow? Only an eagle.

And that smell? Only a bobcat.

Winter came, then melted away, and the wildflowers bloomed under the pine trees. Journey put his nose up in the spring air. If he didn't find a mate soon, he might just give up and go back north to his old pack.

He let out a long howl, broadcasting his presence. To his surprise, for the first time on his long journey, for the first time in almost three years, he heard an answering howl.

"There's a girl wolf!"

Abby stared at the newspaper. A wildlife biologist had taken photos
of Journey and another wolf, smaller than him and jet black. A female.
They were in Oregon, just on the other side of the California border.
Journey didn't go all the way back home! He was still nearby.

With a little detective work scientists figured out that the female wolf
was like Journey. She was a long way from home, a traveler.

Had Journey found what he was looking for?
Did this mean he would stay?

Maybe Journey's story was just beginning.
Maybe wolves were here for good. Maybe
one day Abby and others would actually be
able to see one of Journey's descendants,
or hear wolves howling in the distance,
in the night.

The two wolves settled near a river, in an area where there was space to
run, wildlife to hunt, and no humans. It was just the right place to raise
a family.

That summer when the little pups stumbled out of their den, blinking
in the sunlight, Journey was there beside them.

Along with his mate he caught food for them and played with them, and
as they grew, he taught them how to survive here, in these woods, their
home, this vast stretch of wilderness, where there are not too many
roads and not too many farms—just right for wolves.

THE REAL JOURNEY

OR7 is a real gray wolf who was born into the Imnaha Pack in Northeast Oregon in 2009. In 2011 wildlife biologists fitted the young wolf with a radio tracking collar that would tell them where he was at all times, allowing them to learn more about wolves. He was named OR7 because he was the seventh wolf to be collared in Oregon.

Eight months after being fitted with the collar, OR7 left his pack and began an historic journey that spanned three years and close to two thousand miles. While on this trek OR7 earned a new name, Journey, as a result of a naming contest held by a conservation organization that wanted to draw attention to wolf recovery and make him so famous he wouldn't come to harm. Two children from two different states who participated in the contest submitted the name Journey and won the contest.

Journey was no ordinary wolf. But as it turned out, he wasn't the only wolf to feel the thrill of exploration and to venture far from his birthplace. There was at least one more—the female who became Journey's mate. Although she did not wear a collar, biologists determined, by examining her scat, that she was related to wolves in Northeast Oregon, like Journey, and had probably come from there too.

Journey and his mate created a home near the Rogue River watershed in Oregon, just north of the California border, where the two wolves and their pups became a new pack—the Rogue Pack.

Biologists hope that as the pups grow and leave to form their own packs and more wolves return to this area, it will again become a healthy wolf habitat.

The story of Journey's amazing odyssey will live on as inspiration for wildlife lovers everywhere.

In May 2014 biologists with the US Fish and Wildlife Service discovered this photo of Journey when they checked their remote motion-detection camera, in Jackson County, Oregon. After being strapped to a tree and turned on, the cameras snap photos or video when an animal comes within about fifty feet. Officials periodically download the images. Although the images are sometimes blurry or off-center, they provide valuable information about the locations of packs, the birth of pups, and the animals' health and behavior.

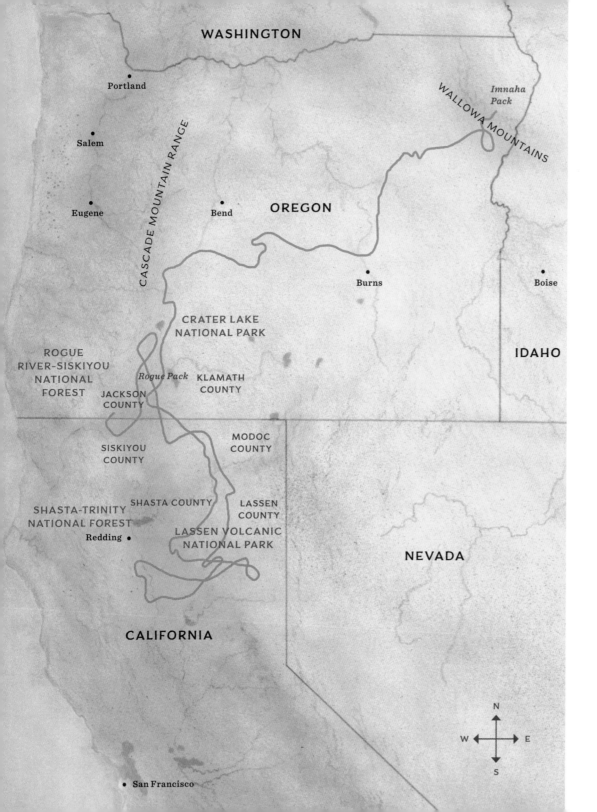

OR7'S JOURNEY

In September 2011 OR7 left the Imnaha Pack in Northeastern Oregon and began the nearly two-thousand-mile journey that made him famous. Because OR7 had been fitted with a radio collar earlier that year, biologists were able to use the readings from the collar to track his travel.

After leaving his pack he spent the next two and a half years wandering alone. During this time he traveled southwest through the state of Oregon, crossed west over the Cascade Mountains, and continued south into California, where he spent over a year.

During 2013 he was detected going back and forth across the Oregon-California border, only to eventually settle in Oregon's Rogue River–Siskiyou National Forest after finding a mate. In the spring of 2014 the two wolves produced a litter of pups, and together they became a new pack: the Rogue Pack.

KEY:

JOURNEY'S ROUTE ————————

This map is an artistic rendering of Journey's route; it is not drawn exactly to scale.

Two of Journey's pups peeked out from inside a hollowed-out log on June 2, 2014. This photo is not from a remote trail camera. Biologist John Stephenson waited for hours with a handheld camera to capture this first photo of the pups.

Unaware that it was looking right into a hidden motion-detection camera, one of Journey's pups seemed to pose for a picture on July 12, 2014. The pup was three months here, the age at which pups abandon the den and begin to accompany their parents on hunting trips.

TIMELINE

1924	1947	1990s	2008	2009
The last wolf in California was shot by a hunter.	The last known wolf bounty in Oregon was collected. (A bounty is money awarded by the government for killing an animal.)	Sixty-six gray wolves captured in Canada were released in Yellowstone National Park and Idaho.	Wolves were confirmed living in Northeastern Oregon.	OR7 was born in Oregon into the Imnaha Pack to a mother named Sophie.

December 28, 2011	January 2012	May 2012	Summer 2012–March 2013	Summer 2013–Spring 2014
OR7 crossed the border into California. He became the first wolf in the state since 1924.	OR7 became known as Journey, a name suggested by two children who participated in the naming contest, one in North Dakota and one in Idaho. On the same day, a newspaper published the first known photo of OR7, taken by a hunter's remote trail camera.	OR7 was observed playing and roaming with coyotes in Modoc County, California.	Biologists tracked OR7 spending time in Northern California's Siskiyou, Shasta, and Lassen Counties.	OR7 seemed to have settled in Southern Oregon, near the California border, in Klamath and Jackson Counties. He was frequently detected crossing the state border into California and then returning to Oregon.

FOR FURTHER READING

DEFENDERS OF WILDLIFE
www.defenders.org/gray-wolf/basic-facts

INTERNATIONAL WOLF CENTER
www.wolf.org/learn/wild-kids/

OREGON DEPARTMENT OF FISH AND WILDLIFE
www.dfw.state.or.us/wolves/rogue_pack.asp

OREGON WILD
www.oregonwild.org/wildlife/wolves/the-journey-of-or7

February 2011
Biologists attached radio collars to several wolves in Oregon, including OR7, to study their migration patterns.

September 10, 2011
OR7 left his pack, a behavior biologists call dispersal (typical for nondominant males).

November–December 2011
OR7 headed into Southern Oregon, then turned west and crossed the Cascade Mountains, becoming the first known wolf in Western Oregon in sixty years.

November 2011
An organization called Oregon Wild launched an art and naming contest intended to draw attention to the wolf recovery program and to make OR7 "too famous to kill."

May 2014
OR7 appeared to have found a companion, a female.

June 2014
Biologists detected at least three pups fathered by OR7. The new family, designated the Rogue Pack, settled in the area around the Rogue River watershed, in Southern Oregon's Rogue River–Siskiyou National Forest.

July 2015
OR7 and his mate produced a second litter of at least two pups.

August 2015
A wolf pack, including five pups, was detected in California's Siskiyou County. The presence of the Shasta Pack makes it more plausible that OR7's adult pups will be able to find mates and continue the repopulation of wolves in Northern California and Southern Oregon.

For my parents, Sally and Roger Bland, and my grandmother, Marjorie Ruess Bland, who gifted me their love of wild things —E. B. S.

To my husband, Randy, for his endless love and support, allowing me to do what I love to do —R. J.

Text copyright © 2016 by Emma Bland Smith
Illustrations copyright © 2016 by Robin James

Manufactured in China by C&C Offset Printing Co. Ltd. Shenzhen, Guangdong Province, in June 2016

Published by Little Bigfoot, an imprint of Sasquatch Books
20 19 18 17 16   9 8 7 6 5 4 3 2 1

Editor: Christy Cox
Production editor: Emma Reh

Library of Congress Cataloging-in-Publication Data is available.

ISBN: 978-1-63217-065-1

Sasquatch Books
1904 Third Avenue, Suite 710
Seattle, WA 98101
(206) 467-4300
www.sasquatchbooks.com
custserv@sasquatchbooks.com

Photo of Journey courtesy of US Fish and Wildlife Service
Photo of Journey's pups in the den, by John Stephenson, courtesy US Fish and Wildlife Service
Photo of Journey's pup courtesy US Fish and Wildlife Service

Journey is a work of fiction. OR7 is a real wolf that did travel from Northern Oregon to Northern California. However, any references to historical events are intended to give this fictional story an historical setting. Other names, characters, and incidents are either the product of the author's imagination or are used fictitiously.

GET MORE OUT OF THIS BOOK

GROUP DISCUSSION

- Before reading the story, ask readers, "What does it mean to be famous?" and "What do you think would make a wolf famous?"

- While reading the story, ask readers about why they think it is important for OR7 to find a mate.

- Discuss how using technology, such as radio collars and the internet, can help animal recovery.

- Discuss why it is beneficial for animals to live in packs. Ask about any disadvantages to living in packs.

INDEPENDENT ACTIVITIES

- Ask readers how wolves and coyotes are similar and how they are different. Have readers use the internet to gather information to write a report comparing these animals, including their size, population, diet, and hunting practices.

- Ask readers to write out a timeline, capturing major events in Journey's life. Have them compare it with a timeline of their lives, noting times when their family has moved or relocated.

- Compare the map in the book to real pictures of wilderness areas and landmarks mentioned in the story found in media searches on the internet.

- Ask readers to write an opinion piece responding to the question, "Do you think it is important to reintroduce wolves into vast wilderness areas with 'not too many roads and not too many farms'?"

GROUP ACTIVITIES

- Ask readers to compare how wolves are portrayed in this story to the traditional wolf themes in folk stories and fables where the wolf is the antagonist, such as in *Little Red Riding Hood*. Have them share their thoughts with each other.

- Without showing the illustration and after reading the sentence "His sharp ears heard a low click, and he turned his head toward the noise," stop and ask readers, "What do you think made the sound?" On the same page ask for the meaning and synonyms of the word *veered*.

- Discuss what readers think a wilderness is by participating in a short collaborative conversation, asking readers to share their thinking with each other.

TEACHER'S GUIDE

The above discussion questions and activities are from our teacher's guide, which is aligned with the Common Core State Standards for English Language Arts and can be adapted to Grades K–5. For the complete guide and a list of the exact standards it aligns with, visit our website: SasquatchBooks.com.